If my teacher went to Mars

Written and Art Directed By

Madison Low

ILLUSTRATION BY @VALENTART_

Copyright © 2018 by Madison Low.

All rights reserved. No part of this book may be reproduced, transmitted, or stored in an information retrieval system in any form or by any means, graphic, electronic, or mechanical, including photocopying, taping, and recording, without prior written permission from the publisher.

First edition 2018

Library of Congress Control Number: 2018912884

ISBN 978-1-7329309-8-8 (paperback)
ISBN 978-1-7329309-9-5 (electronic)

Tellurium Press
340 S Lemon Ave #5151
Walnut CA 91789
United States

Vist us at www.booksbymadison.com

To Mrs. Smith and Mrs. Young for
teaching and inspiring me to do good things.

If my teacher went to Mars,

will she float on a lava river?

If my teacher went to Mars,

will she make a tent?

If my teacher went to Mars,

will she camp with a marshmallow by her side?

If my teacher went to Mars,

will she bring the class pet
parrot along?

If my teacher went to Mars,

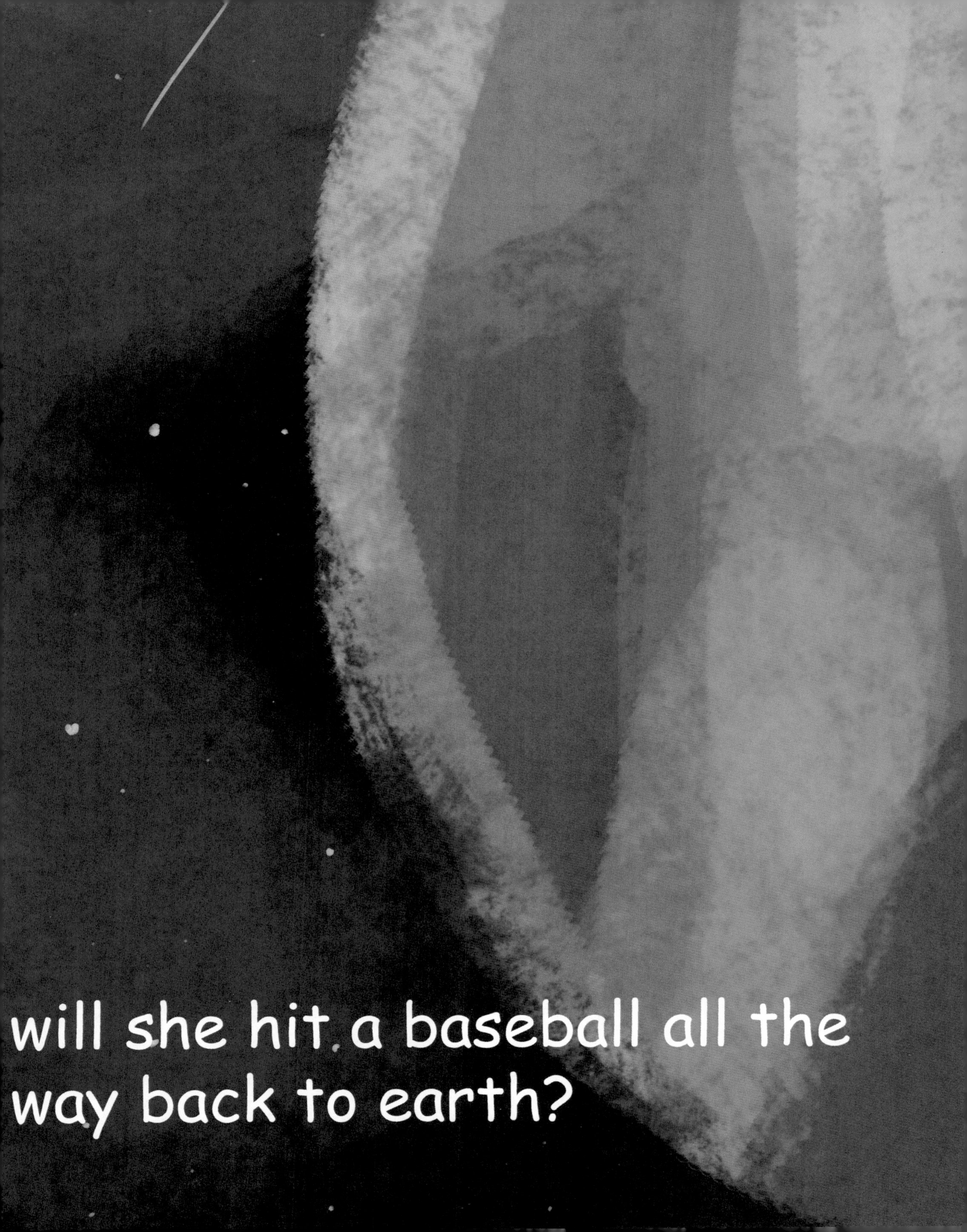

will she hit a baseball all the way back to earth?

If my teacher went to Mars,

will she have her birthday there?

If my teacher
went to Mars,

will she learn to speak alien?

If my teacher went to Mars,

will she teach
little aliens?

If my teacher went to Mars,

will she plant a tree?

If my teacher went to Mars,

will she bring a robot?

If my teacher went to Mars,

she will bring her
students!

Tellurium Press

Vist us at www.booksbymadison.com

Made in the USA
Coppell, TX
09 July 2020